MW00989298

7½ B
1

G.P. Putnam's Sons

New York

Christina Katerina
and the Great Bear Train

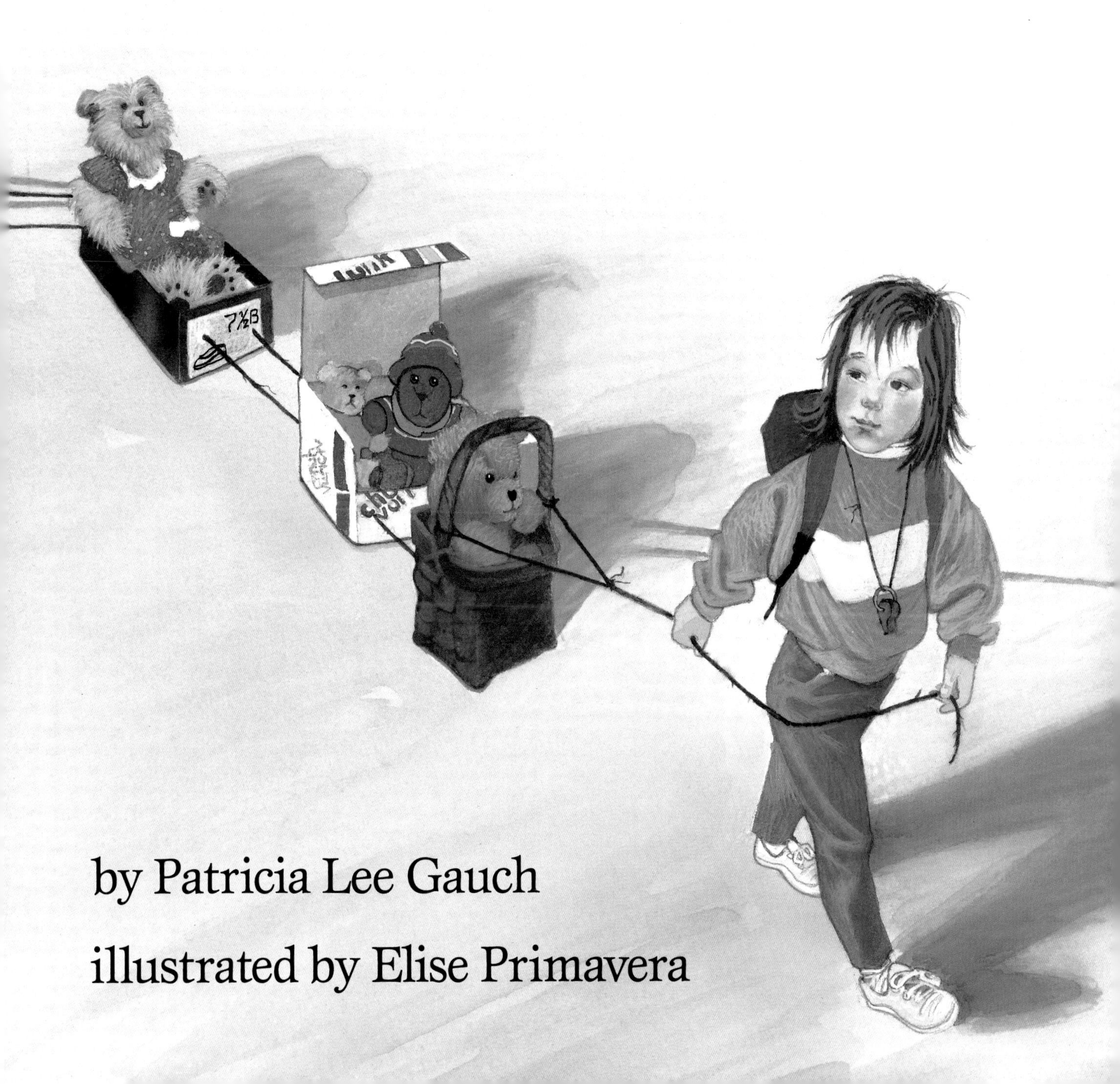

by Patricia Lee Gauch

illustrated by Elise Primavera

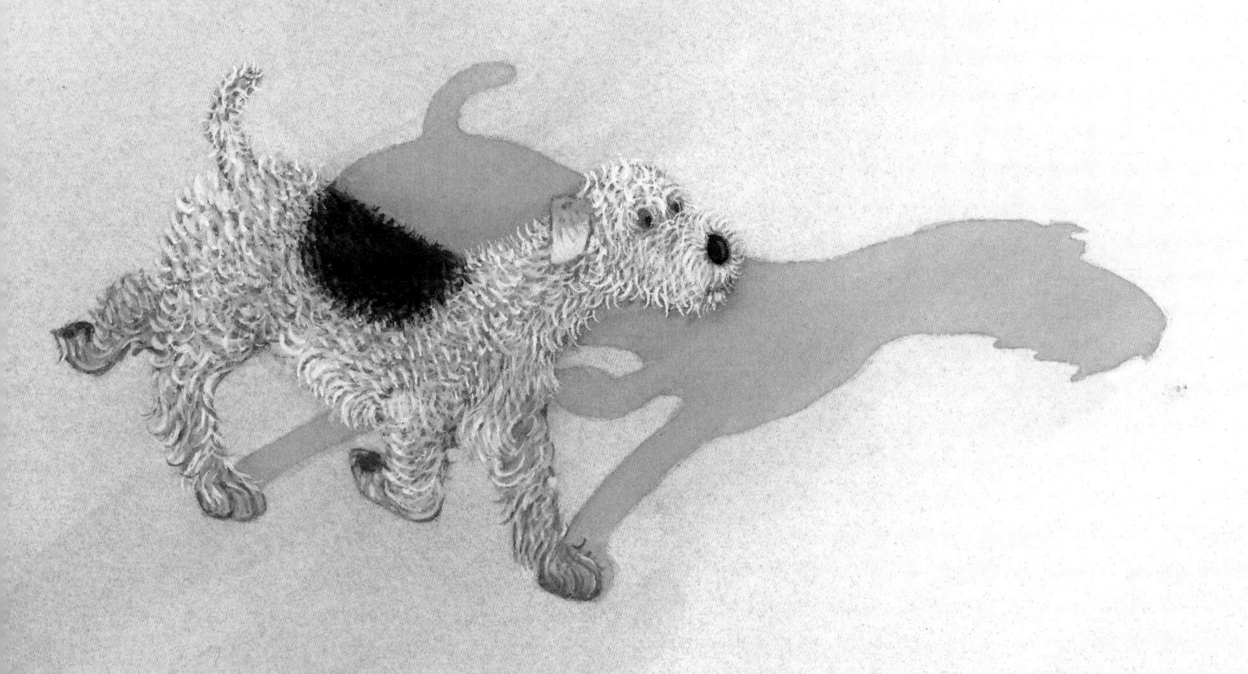

G. P. Putnam's Sons, a division of The Putnam & Grosset Group
200 Madison Avenue, New York, NY 10016
Published simultaneously in Canada
Printed in Hong Kong by South China Printing Co. (1988) Ltd.
The text is set in ITC Garamond Light.

Library of Congress Cataloging-in-Publication Data
Gauch, Patricia Lee.
Christina Katerina and the great bear train/by Patricia Lee Gauch;
illustrated by Elise Primavera.
p. cm.
Summary: Not happy that a new baby sister is coming home from the hospital, Christina Katerina takes her toy bears on a faraway train journey all over the neighborhood.
[1. Teddy bears—Fiction. 2. Railroads—Trains—Fiction.
3. Babies—Fiction.] I. Primavera, Elise, ill. II. Title.
PZ7.G2315Cje 1990 88-28241 CIP AC
[E]—dc19
ISBN 0-399-21623-5

---

10 9 8 7 6 5 4 3 2 1
First Impression

For Judy Murray, a friend—P.L.G.

To my models, Taissa Kachala
and Christopher Doyle—E.P.

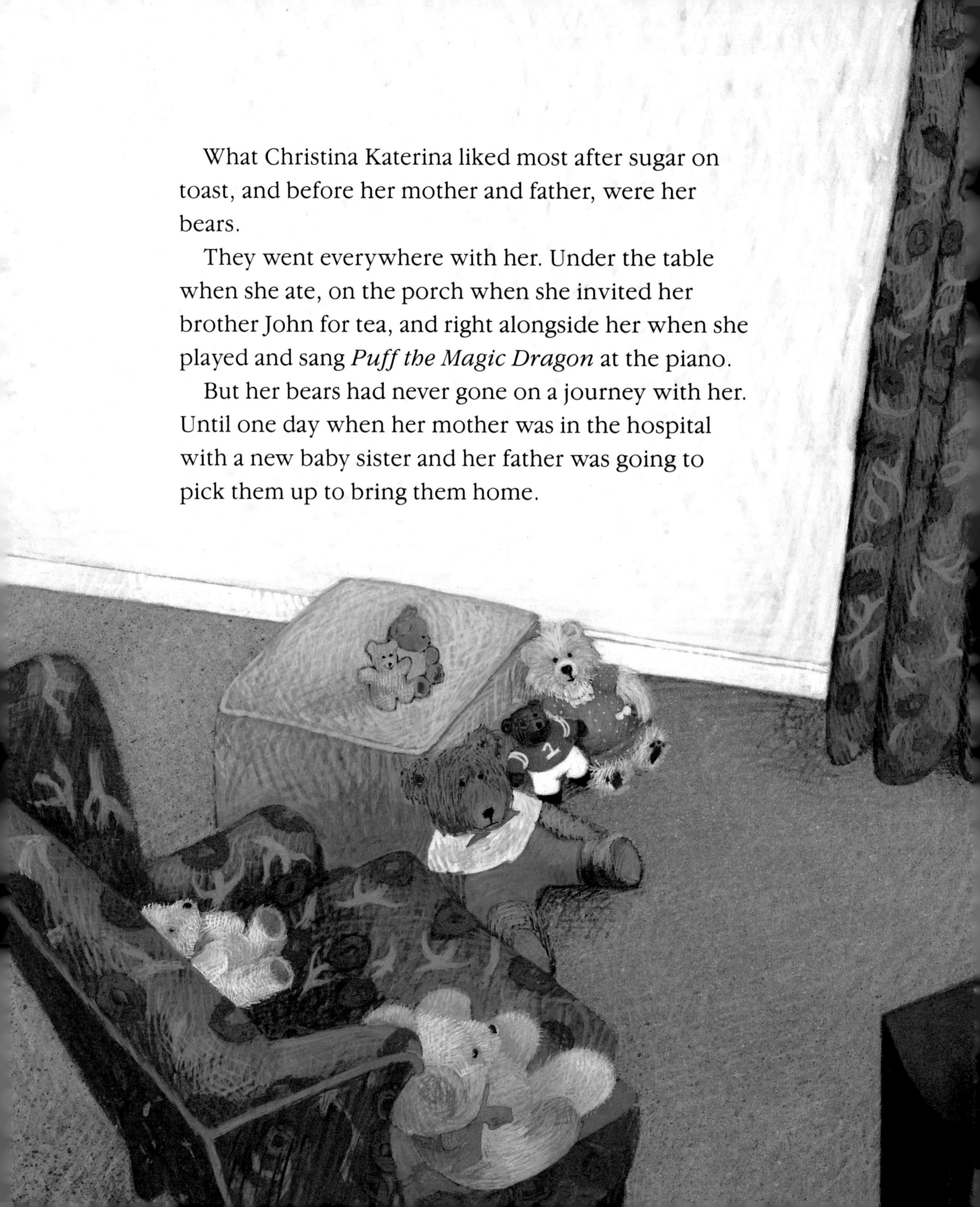

What Christina Katerina liked most after sugar on toast, and before her mother and father, were her bears.

They went everywhere with her. Under the table when she ate, on the porch when she invited her brother John for tea, and right alongside her when she played and sang *Puff the Magic Dragon* at the piano.

But her bears had never gone on a journey with her. Until one day when her mother was in the hospital with a new baby sister and her father was going to pick them up to bring them home.

7½B

"You'll love your baby sister. We'll be back soon," her father said to Christina.

"I don't need a baby sister. We're going on a journey," Christina said to her bears.

"Help your grandmother, Christina," her father said.

"By train," Christina said to her bears.

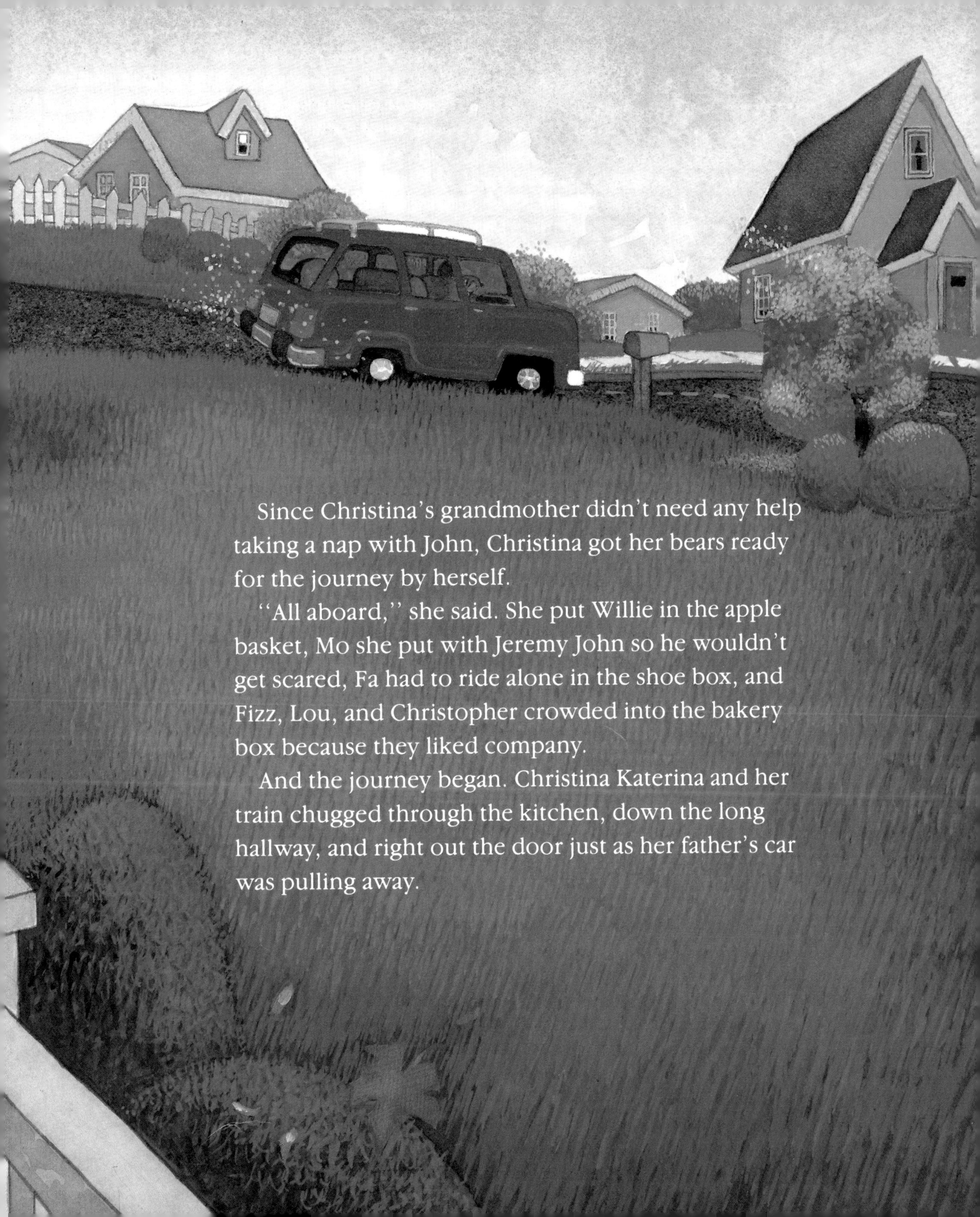

Since Christina's grandmother didn't need any help taking a nap with John, Christina got her bears ready for the journey by herself.

"All aboard," she said. She put Willie in the apple basket, Mo she put with Jeremy John so he wouldn't get scared, Fa had to ride alone in the shoe box, and Fizz, Lou, and Christopher crowded into the bakery box because they liked company.

And the journey began. Christina Katerina and her train chugged through the kitchen, down the long hallway, and right out the door just as her father's car was pulling away.

It was a perfect day for a journey.

Christina Katerina and her train chugged slowly down the walk and right through the lake at the corner. The bears put their paws out for a sip.

She and the bears chugged past Mrs. Jenkins' yard where apples on branches drooped to the ground, and the bears each got to have one.

She and the train coasted in a woosh down the hill where Peter and Charlie were attacking kings and their one million soldiers with tomatoes. Christina and her bears stopped to help.

Peachtree la.

After the battle, Fa climbed in with Mo and Jeremy John and they chugged on down Peachtree Lane. When the road ended, a policeman stopped the cars for the train to cross. Willie waved, but Christina didn't. "On a journey, there's no time for hellos and goodbyes," she said as she chugged across.

When they reached the other side, Peachtree Lane had disappeared and houses with sleepy eyes that Christina and her bears had never seen before blinked at them, and Fa and Lou were not the brave bears they had been.

But Christina was still exactly Christina. "The best sort of journey is a faraway journey," she said and she chugged right on down the street. Left a block, three more blocks to the right, then straight ahead. "We're almost there," she said. "There" was where all good journeys ended.

But then just past a big pine tree, a strange dog with a bandanna around his neck tipped the train, and before Christina could blow the whistle, he ran away with the caboose. "Dragon!" Christina said.

As the train raced past a school yard trying to catch up with its caboose, three boys with not enough teeth started throwing walnuts. "Don't speak to strangers," Christina said to her bears and threw the walnuts back.

Just past a yellow house it started to rain. "Every journey has a little rain," Christina said, but the only bears that were happy were Fizz, Christopher, and Mo who knew how to stay afloat.

Jeremy John was worried that they were lost and that they would never get home. But Christina wasn't. She still had her nose, and she knew that the best thing to do on a faraway journey was to follow it. So she wasn't surprised at all when her nose led her past a yellow house, a field, left three blocks, straight one, and right across the street from Peachtree Lane.

She *was* surprised when she saw a brown speck running down the hill before she could cross the street. It was her father. "Christina!" he said and he hugged her. "Where have you been?"

"On a journey," she said. "But I'm back."

"I'm glad," her father said and he helped the train chug up the hill to Christina's house. And of course Christina and the bears were glad too because Lou was hungry and Fizz had had quite enough company, and Christina knew now that the very best thing about going on a faraway journey was coming home.

Particularly when you had a new baby sister there waiting for you.